兔
Rabbit

虎
Tiger

龍
Dragon

牛
Ox

蛇
Snake

鼠
Rat

馬
Horse

For nearly 5,000 years, the Chinese culture
has organized time in cycles of twelve years.
This Eastern calendar is based upon the movement
of the moon (as compared to the Western which
follows the sun). The zodiac circle symbolizes this.
An animal that has unique qualities represents each year.
Therefore, if you are born in a particular year,
then you share the personality of that animal.
Now people worldwide celebrate this
fifteen-day festival in the early spring and enjoy
the start of another Chinese New Year.

豬
Pig

羊
Sheep

狗
Dog

雞
Rooster

猴
Monkey

To my brother Geoffrey: the one who got the red egg
and was the first rabbit I ever knew.
—O.C.

To Papa: who has always kept the most wonderful garden
that any little bunny would be lucky to find.
To Alexandra: for all her love and patience.
And to my family: for their endless encouragement
and support. I love you all so much.
—J.R.

immedium
Immedium, Inc.   P.O. Box 31846   San Francisco, CA 94131
www.immedium.com

First hardcover edition published 2011.

Edited by Don Menn
Book design by Elaine Chu
Calligraphy by Lucy Chu

Printed in Singapore
10 9 8 7 6 5 4 3 2 1

Chin, Oliver Clyde, 1969-
  The year of the rabbit : tales from the Chinese zodiac / by Oliver Chin ;
illustrated by Justin Roth. -- First hardcover ed.
      p. cm.
  Summary: Rosie the rabbit befriends a boy who leads her on a wild adventure with a tiger. Lists the birth
years and characteristics of individuals born in the Chinese Year of the Rabbit.
  ISBN 978-1-59702-023-7 (hardcover)
  [1. Rabbits--Fiction. 2. Animals--Fiction. 3. Astrology, Chinese--Fiction.] I. Roth, Justin, ill. II. Title.
  PZ7.C44235Yep 2011
  [E]--dc22

2010002440

ISBN 10: 1-59702-023-0
ISBN 13: 978-159702-023-7

The Year of the Rabbit

Tales from the Chinese Zodiac

Written by Oliver Chin
Illustrated by Justin Roth

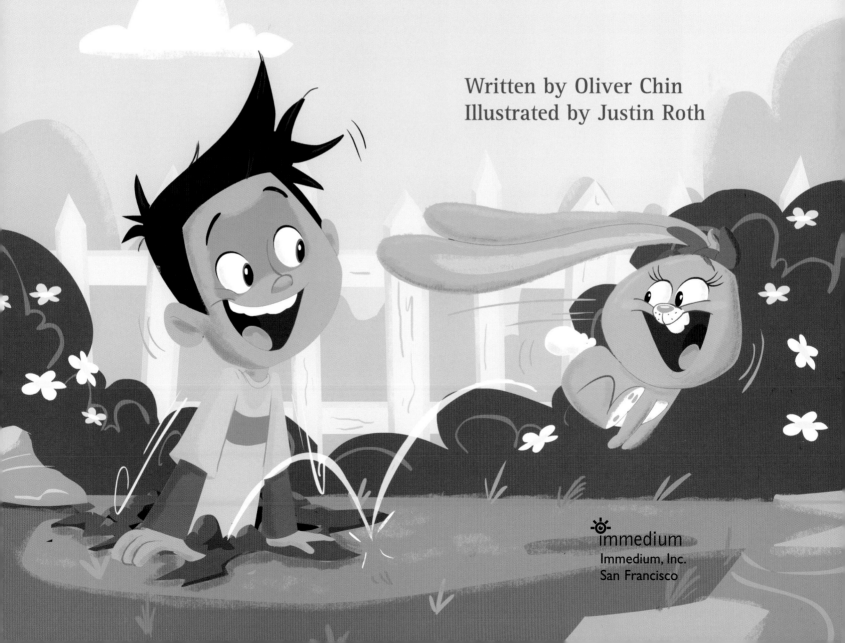

immedium
Immedium, Inc.
San Francisco

A family of rabbits lived underground in a bunch of burrows. Mama and Papa Rabbit introduced their newest baby to everyone. She had soft, hazel-colored fur, and Rosie was her name.

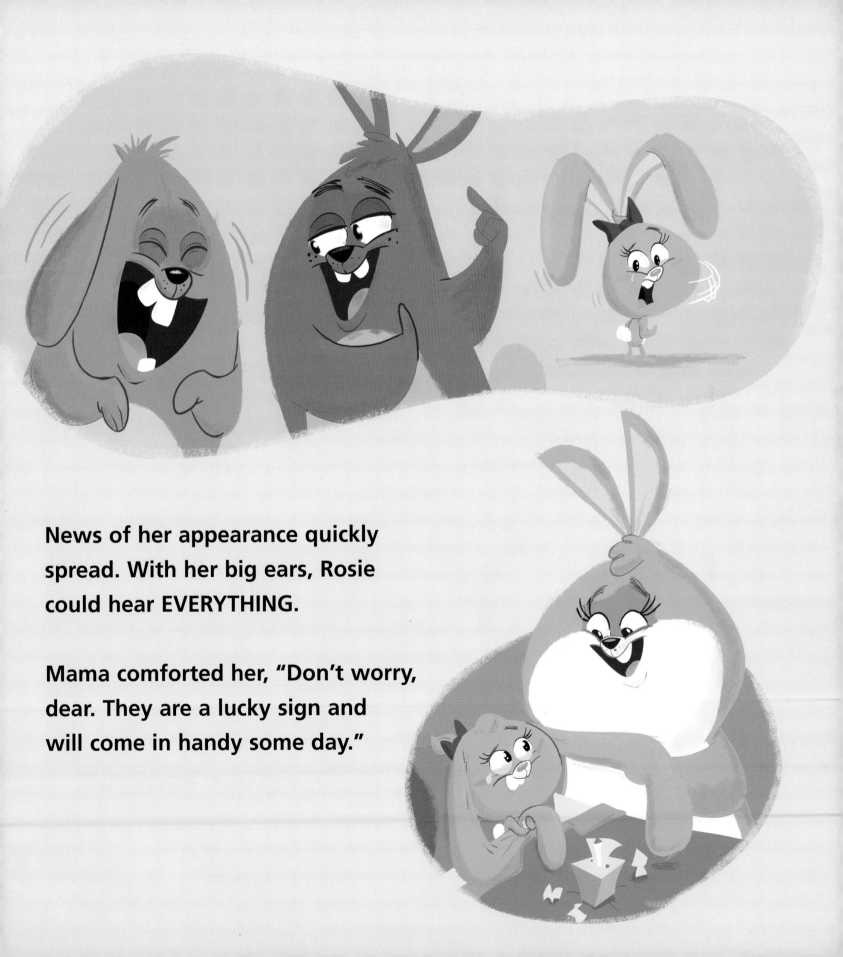

News of her appearance quickly spread. With her big ears, Rosie could hear EVERYTHING.

Mama comforted her, "Don't worry, dear. They are a lucky sign and will come in handy some day."

Rosie had many brothers, sisters, and cousins, such as Velvet the cottontail, Harvey the hare, and Uncle Remus the jackrabbit.

Together they played in the grassy meadow above their home.

However, Rosie thought the grass might be greener elsewhere: **"I want new sights to see and plants to taste."**

Papa warned her, "Be careful what you ask for. Other animals may want you for dinner."

Then one morning, a stranger walked past. He bragged, "I found a patch of a yummy food nearby."

"There's no such thing as a free lunch," scoffed Papa. But Rosie convinced her playmates to go find it.

As Rosie hopped after her siblings, Mama called,
"For Pete's sake, where are you going?"

Following the traveler's directions, they came to a
picket fence. There they saw an incredible sight.

On the other side was a beautiful garden with a rainbow of fruits and vegetables. In the distance, a woman and a child tended the crops. Making sure the coast was clear, the rabbits dug beneath the gate.

Delicious smells lured the rabbits forward. In the garden, they marveled at rows of basil, bok choy, and brussels sprouts. Soon Rosie and her pals were rolling in parsley and clover.

Suddenly a call rang out, "Stop, you varmints!"
The gardeners ran toward them, and the startled
rabbits scampered back to the fence. Yet Rosie took
another nibble and was the last to leave.

She dove under the gate,
and her ears got stuck.
"Help!" she cried.

Her friends returned to
lend a paw, but Rosie
was tugged backwards.
She had been caught!

"Po-Po, you got one!" the boy laughed.
"Hey, this bunny looks kind of funny."

The rabbit said, **"Hi, my name is Rosie."**

The woman smiled, "Jai, after all this running,
I have worked up quite an appetite."

Yet Jai pleaded, "Oh, grandma, can I keep her as a pet? Please?"

"Ok, but you take care of her," answered Po-Po. In the barn, he put a bed of hay in a wooden hutch. Once inside, Rosie dined on lettuce and fell asleep after her long day.

The next morning, curious neighbors came to see Jai's new pet. Were the old tales about rabbits true? Offering some vegetables, the sheep wondered, "Do you like carrots the best?"

"I like beets better," replied Rosie.

Another came forward and patted Rosie's paw. The pig explained, "They say you rub a rabbit's foot for good luck."

"Ha, ha! Stop that!" giggled Rosie. "It tickles!"

Then the ox gave Rosie a basket of eggs and the horse asked, "Can you color them so we can play hide and seek?"

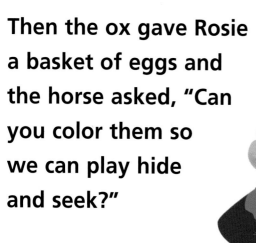

Instead, Rosie brought them to the rooster and said, **"I think this is your job."**

Meanwhile, Jai wanted to try the magic trick of pulling a rabbit from a hat.

Many times he tapped the hat with a stick and announced, "A-bra-ca-da-bra."

But Rosie could never hide her ears.

This rabbit wasn't what they expected at all. "You are a funny bunny," concluded Jai. Rosie thought they were odd too, but she did enjoy new food to eat, friends to meet, and games to play.

Indeed she had grown to like Jai, his neighbors, and the garden. But she did miss her family at home.

Later that night, she heard footsteps approaching in the darkness. It was Mama and Papa!

Mama whispered, "We've come to spring you from here."

Unlocking the cage door, Papa told her, "Hop to it, girl!"

In Rosie's haste, one of her ears brushed against the nose of the sleeping dog.

Ah-choo!

Jai woke up and yelled,
"Rosie? Hey, come back here!"

A moment later, Po-Po called,
"Jai, where are you?" But he
and the dog had run off already.

At last, Rosie and her parents arrived home safely. Jai hollered, "Where did that rascal go?" He and the dog startled a tiger lounging close by.

"Boy, I am hungry," the tiger thought. He crept forward for a closer look and an easy meal.

Noticing the big cat, the dog bolted off. "What's the matter?" Jai shouted.

"It's about time," muttered Papa.
"Those pesky critters left."

But Rosie heard Jai's cry. She peeked
outside to see Jai running into the
woods. Oh, no! Who could save him?

Rosie had an idea. Following the sound of the footsteps, she quickly raced down the tunnel. Mama asked, "Now what are you up to?"

"Don't worry about me!" replied Rosie.
"I can take care of myself!"

In the forest, the hunter cornered the boy. Just then Rosie popped out from a nearby hole and caught the tiger by the tail. She picked Jai up and bounded away.

Rosie zigged and zagged, but could not shake the tiger. Finally, she leapt over a log and told Jai to lie low.

Thrown off the trail, the cat wondered where the bouncing bunny went.

The crouching tiger chuckled as it spotted the hidden rabbit. "Aha! I got you!" the beast growled and grabbed Rosie's big ears with his sharp claws.

Ouch! They belonged to someone else! The dragon was steamed that its beauty sleep had been interrupted. So the sorry tiger fled with the angry serpent hot on his heels.

"We escaped by a hair," sighed Rosie. Their happy families agreed, when they found the children soon thereafter.

Jai thanked Rosie, "Well, zip-a-dee-doo-dah! You really are a good luck charm."

After saving each other's skins, Jai and Rosie became best buddies.

They traded visits and special favors that faithful friends freely give.

And Rosie continued to be a little different than others expected.

Indeed Rosie was like a special flower that shone with a warm and lovely heart. And everyone around the meadow called it an extraordinary Year of the Rabbit.

兔
Rabbit
1915, 1927, 1939, 1951, 1963, 1975, 1987, 1999, 2011, 2023

People born in the Year of the Rabbit are amiable and gentle. Known for having fine taste, they are nimble and resourceful too. But they can be wary and sometimes too clever for their own good. Yet rabbits are both fortunate and forgiving, so count yourself lucky to have friends like them.